Library of Congress Cataloging-in-Publication Data

Spetter, Jung-Hee, 1969-
    [Lentekriebels. English]
    Lily and Trooper's spring / Jung-Hee Spetter. — 1st American ed.
        p.   cm.
    Summary: A little girl and her dog spend a spring day outdoors
    with the birds, cows, sheep, pigs, and ducks.
    ISBN 1-886910-36-7 (hardcover)
    [1. Spring—Fiction. 2. Dogs—Fiction. 3. Animals—Fiction.] I. Title.
        PZ7.S7515Lit   1999
        [E]—dc21   98-27973

Copyright © 1998 by Lemniscaat b.v. Rotterdam
Originally published in the Netherlands under the title *Lentekriebels*
by Lemniscaat b.v. Rotterdam
Printed and bound in Belgium

First American edition

Jung-Hee Spetter

Lily and Trooper's Spring

Front Street & Lemniscaat

Asheville, North Carolina

"Trooper, listen! The birds are really singing today."

"Trooper! It's spring!"

"We're going on a picnic, a picnic, a picnic . . ."

"... and we'll have a cup of tea."

"Moooo!"

"Run, Trooper!"

"Trooper, climb!"

"Phew! Let's get cleaned up."

"Do you want to swing too, Trooper?"

"Let's go higher!"

"Whoops!" – "Woof!"

Ooomph!

"Baaaaaaa!"

Sploosh! "Yuck!"

"Oink!"

"Oink? Oink?"

"Sorry, I just wanted to hold her!"

"Let's get cleaned up, Trooper."

"We're going for a ride. You're the baby."

"Quack! Quack quack! Quack quack quack!"

"We'll take you to the park. Won't we, Trooper?"

"Bye bye." – "Woof woof!" – "Quack quack!"

"Bath time again, Trooper."

"Good night, Trooper." – "Woof!"